IVOR

the engine

The Dragon

Story by OLIVER POSTGATE

Pictures by PETER FIRMIN

POOP POOP POOPETY-POOP went Ivor's whistle as they rounded the bend above Llaniog. He wasn't whistling a warning. He wasn't whistling a signal. He was whistling for the joy of being alive and steaming, for the joy of seeing the cows in the fields and the sheep on the hills and the big wheel of the Pit spinning in the sunshine.

"See that hill on the left," said Jones the Steam, Ivor's driver, "that is called Smoke

Hill. Some say it was once a volcano."

POOP POOP POOP!

"What? Smoke? Why so there is!"

There was!

Ivor stopped beside Smoke Hill and Jones ran up the hill. The smoke was coming from under the loose stones on top of the hill. He touched one. It was very hot.

Jones fetched the big fire-tongs and began to shift the stones.

Under the stones he found something
amazing.

Red-hot it was and big as a Rugby football.

Very gingerly Jones lifted it with the
tongs and carried it down to Ivor.

"What do you reckon that is?" he asked,
placing it gently on the footplate.

POOP . . . Ivor didn't know.

"No, neither do I," replied Jones. "I
reckon we had better take it up and show it
to Mr Dinwiddy. He's a gold miner. If
anybody knows about rocks, he does."

So they took the red-hot object up to the
gold mine.

Mr Dinwiddy looked at it wisely and prodded it with a bony finger.

PSSST . . . "Owch! It's red-hot!"

"Yes, we know that," said Jones. "What we don't know is what to do with it."

"I reckon that thing is red-hot because it's supposed to be red-hot so you'd better put it back in the red-hot hole where you found it." said Mr Dinwiddy.

POOP POOP POOPETY POOP

"Oh yes, it's time for Ivor's choir practice. I'll put it in Ivor's firebox. We can take it back later."

That thing, whatever it was, in Ivor's firebox was as hot as a hundredweight of best coal. Ivor steamed like the wind down to Grumbly Town where Evans the Song, the choirmaster and the Grumbly and District Choral Society were waiting.

"Ah, there you are Ivor," said Mr Evans in his tuneful voice. "Well, now we are all met, shall we sing?"

Evans the Song lifted his little white stick and they began their choir practice.

TAP TAP TAP

Evans tapped on his music stand.

"Just a moment please!"

The choir stopped singing but from somewhere a fine treble voice continued the song.

"Somebody is still singing!" said Evans.

He looked around. It was almost as if the singing came from inside Ivor's boiler.

"The thing!" shouted Jones. He whipped open Ivor's fire door.

"What thing?" asked Evans the Song.

"It's broken, look!" said Jones.

On the red-hot coal they saw a heap of pieces, just like the shell of a huge egg.

"Do you know 'Land of My Fathers'?"
"Eh?"
They looked up.

There, looking out of Ivor's funnel was a dragon. Not one of your lumping great fairy-tale dragons, it was a small, trim, heraldic Welsh dragon, glowing red-hot and smiling.

"Do you know 'Land of My Fathers?'"
Evans the Song stopped gaping and remembered his manners.

"Why yes, of course, of course. And very

suitable to the occasion, if I may say so.
Come, Ladies and Gentlemen . . . er, Engines
and Dragons, Land of My Fathers, if you
please."

They sang.

They sang most beautifully as always, and
the dragon's voice was the clearest and most
beautiful of all. Their song rang through
the streets and the houses and the gasworks
and echoed from the hills, golden in the
light of the evening sun.

Ivor's firebox is really a very comfortable place for a red-hot dragon to roost.

Idris . . . that was the dragon's name . . . was quite pleased to move in and travel about with Ivor but Dai Station, the Station master, did not agree. He fetched the Book of Regulations and a large cat-basket.

"Conveyance of Livestock," he read. "All livestock to be conveyed in the proper container . . . So, if you please, Mr Dragon."

"You want me to climb into the basket?" asked the dragon anxiously.

"I am afraid I must insist," said Dai.

The dragon climbed into the basket.
It burst into flames.
"I was afraid that would happen."
"Fire! Fire!" shouted Dai and he ran for
the fire-bucket.
"No! No!" shouted the dragon. "Not water!
Water is certain death to dragons!"
Dai did not hear him. He threw the bucket
of water but the dragon had shot straight
up into the sky like a rocket.
"Oh Dai, you could have killed him!"
cried Jones. "Where is he now?"
With his little wings buzzing, the cooling

dragon was circling the town to find a red-hot place. He felt the blast of heat from Eli the Baker's oven and dived straight down the chimney.

"He's at Eli the Baker's!" shouted Jones "Come on Dai, run!"

Eli the Baker opened his oven door and pulled out a line of hot loaves. He blinked short-sightedly at the last one.

"There's fancy bread now!"

"That's not bread! That's our dragon!"
shouted Jones, bursting in through the door.

"Oooh brrrr! I'm cold!" wailed the dragon.
Quick as a flash Eli opened the furnace.

"In you get!"

"Oh thank you! Oh that's better!" sighed
the dragon as he settled on the blazing coal.

"There's the trouble Eli," explained Jones,

"Idris is a red-hot dragon. He has to be kept red-hot all the time."

"And livestock has to be conveyed in the proper container," said Dai, "only what is the proper container for a red-hot dragon?"

Eli the Baker thought for a moment. Then he smiled a broad smile.

"I might have sold it for scrap or thrown it away but, no, I said to myself, one day somebody will need it."

"What are you talking about?" said Jones.

"Come and see," said Eli.

Under the shed roof at the back of Eli's

yard was a . . . what was it?

"Looks like a tricycle," said Dai, "but there's a coke stove on the front."

"Chestnuts!" shouted Jones.

"That's right," said Eli. "I used to sell roast chestnuts but I gave that up years ago. I thought we could make the fire . . ."

"Yes!"

". . . and your dragon could . . ."

"Of course!"

". . . while you pedal it along!"

"Marvellous!"

So that's what they did, and Jones

pedalled the smoking tricycle through
Llaniog Town.

"You selling chestnuts now?" called Mrs
Williams the Post Office.

"No, just dragons!" laughed Jones.

"There's enterprising for you!" said Mrs
Williams the Post Office.

You might think a red-hot dragon about
the place would be a nuisance but Dai and
Jones soon got used to looking after him
and he was really no trouble.

In fact he could be useful, like the time
when the whole of the choir decided to go
to Mrs Thomas's fish and chip shop.

"Sixteen cod and chips please, Mrs Thomas," said Evans the Song.

"Sixteen?" wailed poor Mrs Thomas. "The gas burner is playing up. I can't seem to get the fryer hot!"

So there was only one thing to do. Idris is a bit shy usually but this was an emergency. Jones told him what had happened and he left Ivor's firebox and flew down to the shop.

"What's this?" cried Mrs Thomas in alarm.

"Just our friend Idris the dragon," said
Evans soothingly. "He will oblige us with a
few fiery breaths and then you will have fire
and warmth all glowing under your fryer
and we shall have fish and chips."

And so it was.

Idris sat under the fryer and blew and
blew. Soon the fat began to sizzle and soon
the shop was full of the lovely smell of fish
and chips and the happy sound of eating.

"I say, Jones," said Evans. "Listen to what's written in my bit of paper!

DRAGONS AT LLANIOG
Unconfirmed reports have been received that a genuine Welsh Dragon has been sighted at Llaniog. The Antiquarian Society states that its representative is to make an immediate investigation . . .

There Idris! You are going to be famous!"

"NO!" cried Idris. "No! Dragons are mythical! No, I must not be investigated! No! No! No!"

With a whistle of red-hot wings Idris was away through the window and gone.

"Well, Ladies and Gentlemen," announced Evans the Song. "I think we haven't seen any dragons, isn't it?"

"Dragons?" said the choir. "What dragons? Lovely fish and chips Mrs Thomas!"

Jones the Steam ran back to Ivor on the
siding. He opened the firebox door. Idris was
not in there.

"Oh Ivor," shouted Jones, "Idris has flown!
The newspaper says he is to be investigated
and he doesn't want to be. Come on! Let's
see if he's in the ash heap by the shed!"

Idris was not in the ash heap. He was not

in Eli's furnace. He was not in the chestnut
barrow. There was no sign of him anywhere.

"Oh I do hope he has found somewhere
hot," sighed Jones, "Oh I do wish we knew
where he has got to!"

He went home that night feeling very sad
and worried.

The next morning, as Jones was talking to

Dai Station on the platform, P.C. Gregory
rode up on his bike.

"Have you seen the dragon?" shouted
Jones.

"Ssssh!" hissed the policeman. "There's a
lady in the town asking for you. Very posh
she is. I think she is the Investigation!"

"Oh dear," muttered Jones, "I'm no good
at telling lies. If she asks me I shall tell
her everything!"

"Aha!" came a well-bred yell from behind him.

Jones spun round. There was Mrs Griffiths of the Antiquarian Society. She was a large lady in a hat.

"Aha!" she hooted, "You must be Mr Jones the Engine driver."

"Yes, I must," said Jones reluctantly. "And this is Ivor. Say hallo to the lady, Ivor!"

Ivor was silent.

"Ivor?" said the lady, puzzled, "which of you gentlemen is Ivor?"

"The engine, Madam," whispered P.C. Gregory.

"Does he always speak to it?"

"Oh yes Madam, we don't take any notice of that," said P.C. Gregory.

Mrs Griffiths gulped and spoke again.

"The dragon," she began, "I hear that you have sighted a dragon . . ."

"Sighted!" cried Jones, "Ivor hatched it from an egg and he fried fish and chips for us at Mrs Thomas's. Sixteen cod and chips!"

"Sixteen?"

"That's right, and he sang like an angel right out of Ivor's funnel, didn't he Ivor?"

Ivor did not answer.

"Oh come on Ivor!"

Ivor remained silent.

"I am very sorry," said Jones, "Ivor isn't usually so rude."

"Well, never mind, never mind!" said Mrs Griffiths, "I am sure everything is all right really."

"Everything is not all right!" said Jones, beginning to feel angry, "We have lost our

dragon!"

"Ah well, you know how it is with dragons," said Mrs Griffiths soothingly. "Here today and gone tomorrow!"

"Is it indeed?" said Jones. "I can tell you we shall miss him."

"We shall all miss him!" sighed Mrs Griffiths.

"But you have never met him!" shouted Jones.

Mrs Griffiths backed away. This Mr Jones who talked to railway engines and said he

had a dragon to cook fish and chips was
obviously barmy.

"Good Morning everybody!" she yelled
and trotted briskly back to her car.

"What a very strange lady!" said Jones.

Dai and P.C. Gregory were falling about
with laughter.

"You are the one that's strange!" laughed
P.C. Gregory. "Talking to railway engines!
Whoever heard of such a thing!"

"Well I reckon that is the end of the
investigation," said Dai, thankfully. "It's

about time you and Ivor did some work. It's
Grumbly gasworks today."

POOP . . . CHUFF CHUFF CHUFF.

Off they went on their day's work.

Quite an ordinary day's work it was, coal
for the gasworks, tomatoes and potatoes for
Mr Davies the greengrocer, half a mowing
machine for Mr Pugh at Tewyn Farm.

As they rolled homeward at the end of the

day Jones felt tired and still very worried.

"If only we knew where he was."

PSSSST . . . Ivor jammed on his brakes.

They were by Smoke Hill.

Jones ran up and turned over the hot stones.

In the red-hot centre of the hill he saw a curled-up bundle of scales and claws.

Idris was fast asleep.

Jones put back the stones and walked quietly back to Ivor.

"That's the best place for him I reckon," he said. "We'll drop in a bag or two of coal now and then if the weather goes cold. Come on Ivor! Time to go home."

POOP . . . CHUFF CHUFF CHUFF . . .

Jones the Steam put Ivor to bed in his shed and went home to tea as if nothing had happened.

This edition published 1994 by Diamond Books
77-85 Fulham Palace Road, Hammersmith London W6 8JB

First published by Picture Lions 1979
14 St James's Place, London SW1

© text and illustrations Oliver Postgate and Peter Firmin 1979

Printed in Slovenia

ISBN 0 261 66 571-5